Almost Famous Daisy!

Richard Kidd

Paintings
Artists
CF

FRANCES LINCOLN

GRAND
PAINTING COMPETITION

on the theme of

My Favourite Things

All paintings must be submitted no later than Sunday, April 1st and must be all your own work.

The judges' decision will be final

Dear Mum and Dad,

We're off to find my favourite things!
We' re off to paint the world!
I know you will be so proud of me
if my picture wins a prize in the contest.
Don't worry, Duggie and I will send you
postcards from all the places we visit.

Love,

Daisy

Daisy and Duggie arrived in France on Monday, and by evening
they were in Saint Rémy. By the time Daisy had unpacked,
it was dark, and an owl was hooting in the almond trees.
She and Duggie climbed to the top of the hill.
They could almost touch the stars! Daisy felt so inspired,
she got out her paints, set up her easel and started work.

CARTE POSTALE

Saint Rémy, Monday

Dear Mum and Dad,

I painted some brilliant stars
this evening. They look almost as
good as the swirling stars on
the other side of this postcard.
If Van Gogh can do it, so can I!
But perhaps the judges would prefer
something more down to earth ...

Dizzily,   Daisy

The Starry Night (1889) Vincent van Gogh

HÔTEL
Claude

27

On Tuesday, Daisy and Duggie went on to Rouen
and found a hotel right in the middle of town.
Everything was rather grey and it looked like rain,

so they stayed in and Daisy began to paint the view from her window - a huge church called Rouen Cathedral.

Rouen, Tuesday

Dear Mum and Dad,

Rouen Cathedral is really impressive
and so is Monet's painting of it
(see other side of postcard). I've had
to paint my picture really fast,
because the light keeps changing.
Maybe I'll stand a better chance
if I stick to landscapes.

Decidedly,   **Daisy**

MUSÉE DES BEAUX-ARTS, ROUEN.

ROUEN TOURS

FRANCE

Hotel Daisy

Rouen Cathedral, the Portal and the Tour Saint-Romain:
Morning Effect, Harmony in White
(1893) CLAUDE MONET

Daisy and Duggie caught a train to Russia, and by Wednesday they were settled into an inn at Vitebsk. Daisy fell in love with Russia - it was so poetic.

She could smell the pine forest and hear the geese honking. Duggie felt poetic too, and chased squirrels. Out came the canvas and paints once more.

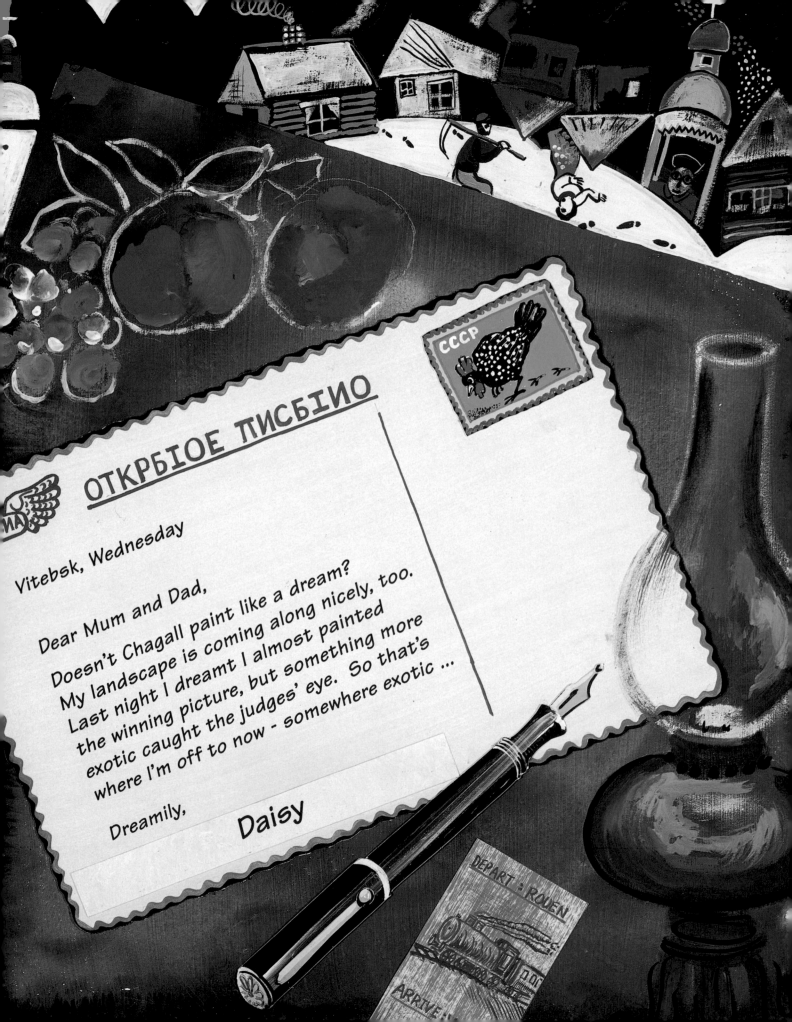

ОТКРЫОЕ ПИСБИПО

Vitebsk, Wednesday

Dear Mum and Dad,

Doesn't Chagall paint like a dream?
My landscape is coming along nicely, too.
Last night I dreamt I almost painted
the winning picture, but something more
exotic caught the judges' eye. So that's
where I'm off to now - somewhere exotic ...

Dreamily,

Daisy

The Poet Reclining (1915) MARC CHAGALL

Thursday - and Daisy and Duggie were in paradise!
Polynesia was lovely and hot, with big bright parrots,
strange scents, whispering waves and friendly people.
It took Daisy's breath away. Soon she was busy painting.

Les Artistes des Mers du Sud.

Tahiti, Thursday

Dear Mum and Dad,

The tropics are gorgeous, and so are
Gauguin's colours! He really knows
how to paint the good life.
But good just isn't good enough for me.
I want to be the best.
I want excitement, action ...

Determinedly,

Daisy

TAHITI

Where do we come from? What are we? Where are we going? (1897) Paul Gauguin

Daisy and Duggie flew to Wyoming, U.S.A.
The wind whistled from one end of the prairie to the other.
As Daisy tried to paint, everything got blown about.

BLUE POLES
RANCH

WALL STREET JOURNAL
NEW YORK
ART PRICES
PLUMMET
30TH
MARCH

Whoops! Her easel fell over.
Splat! Her paint-pots went flying.
Her picture was really looking action-packed.

JACK 1

Duggie's
Favourite

DUGGIE

Blue Poles (1952) JACKSON POLLOCK

New York, Friday

Dear Mum and Dad,

Stopped off here on our way home. I've just seen a great Jackson Pollock picture in a gallery window.

It seems that the world is full of
famous painters - so why not me too?
If only I could find my favourite things.
See you soon.
Duggie is longing for his bone and basket.

Doggedly,

Daisy

DAISY!

Saturday

At last Daisy and Duggie were home!
Her Mum and Dad were so pleased to
see them. They had kept all Daisy's
picture postcards pinned to the notice
board in the kitchen.

Daisy thought her room looked different.
Or was she just seeing it with new eyes?
Little things reminded her of all
the wonderful places she had visited.
It wasn't long before she realised that
her favourite things had been at home
all the time.

Later, her Mum and Dad heard the clatter
of brushes and the squidge of paint.
They peeped through the window and saw
Daisy busy at work on another painting.
She finished it just before bedtime.

buy

milk
biscuits
dog food

SAVE
2p

It was the best painting Daisy had ever done.
Fame at last ... well, almost.
Her Mum and Dad were so proud - and so was Duggie!

About the artists

VINCENT VAN GOGH, 1853-1890 *Dutch artist*

In 1888, after painting for a couple of years in Paris,
van Gogh moved to the South of France. There he started
to produce the thick-brushed, brilliantly-coloured paintings
which have made him a legend. He painted his best-loved
works - *Cornfield and Cypress Trees*, *Starry Night* and
Sunflowers - in the two years before he died.

CLAUDE MONET, 1840-1926 *French artist*

Monet's atmospheric landscapes painted during the 1860s
have earned him a reputation as one of the founders
of the Impressionist movement. In 1883, Monet created a
beautiful garden in Giverny which inspired some of his
greatest paintings.

MARC CHAGALL, 1887-1985 *Russian artist*

Born in Vitebsk, in a country known today as Belarus,
Chagall was an experimental painter influenced
by the Cubist art movement in Paris, but his paintings also
reflect his Jewish upbringing and the influence of Russian
folk art. As well as painting pictures, he illustrated books,
designed stained glass and worked as a theatrical designer
in Russia, France and the United States.

PAUL GAUGUIN, 1848-1903 *French artist*

Brought up in Peru, Gauguin worked with the
Impressionists in Paris. In 1891 he went to Tahiti and
spent the rest of his life painting the exotic images
whose decorative lines and flat bright colours have made
him famous.

JACKSON POLLOCK, 1912-1956 *American artist*

Born in Wyoming, Pollock worked in New York,
where he became a central figure in the art movement
known as Abstract Expressionism. The drip-painting
and action-painting methods he used to create his
large canvases have strongly influenced modern
American painting.